THOMAS KINKADE.
Painter of Light

Silent Night

Thomas Kinkade Studios

HarperCollinsPublishers

A Parachute Press Book

Sometimes I feel that the most poignant hours of the holiday season are not Christmas Day, but Christmas Eve. In the quiet evening before the day's celebration begins, a peaceful stillness descends from the heavens. Homes are filled with warmth and anticipation as families gather to share the joy of Christmas morning.

No other carol sets the tone for this holy evening quite like "Silent Night." It speaks to the immense power of that special moment—the night of Jesus' birth. And so, in this book, scenes of more recent silent nights still glow with the timeless message of love and promise from that miraculous evening so long ago.

I hope that you and your family will enjoy this book every year on Christmas Eve, always remembering that God's presence can be felt in our lives today just as it was on the day Christ was born.

Merry Christmas!

Thomas Kinkade

Silent night, holy night,
All is calm, all is bright

Round yon virgin mother and child.
Holy infant, so tender and mild,

Sleep in heavenly peace,
Sleep in heavenly peace.

Silent night, holy night,
Shepherds quake at the sight;

Glories stream from heaven afar,
Heavenly hosts sing Alleluia!
Christ the Savior is born,
Christ the Savior is born!

Silent night, holy night,
Son of God, love's pure light;

Radiant beams from thy holy face
With the dawn of redeeming grace,

Jesus, Lord, at thy birth,
Jesus, Lord, at thy birth.

Silent night, holy night,
Wondrous star, lend thy light;
With the angels let us sing
Alleluia to our King;

Christ the Savior is born,
Christ the Savior is born!

Silent Night

Words by Joseph Mohr

Music by Franz Gruber

Si - lent night, ho - ly night, All is calm, all is bright

Round yon vir - gin moth - er and child. Ho - ly in - fant, so ten - der and mild,

Sleep in heav - en - ly peace,___ Sleep in heav - en - ly peace.___

Silent night, holy night,
Shepherds quake at the sight;
Glories stream from heaven afar,
Heavenly hosts sing Alleluia!
Christ the Savior is born,
Christ the Savior is born!

Silent night, holy night,
Son of God, love's pure light;
Radiant beams from thy holy face
With the dawn of redeeming grace,
Jesus, Lord, at thy birth,
Jesus, Lord, at thy birth.

Silent night, holy night,
Wondrous star, lend thy light;
With the angels let us sing
Alleluia to our King;
Christ the Savior is born,
Christ the Savior is born!

Silent Night
All artwork © 2006 by Thomas Kinkade Studios, Morgan Hill, CA
A Parachute Press Book

Manufactured in China

Library of Congress Cataloging-in-Publication Data is available.
ISBN-10: 0-06-078743-0 (trade bdg.) — ISBN-13: 978-0-06-078743-1 (trade bdg.)

Typography by Jeanne L. Hogle
1 2 3 4 5 6 7 8 9 10

First Edition